Notch The Plan

NOTCHIN' BOOTS SERIES

NATALIE ARTHUR

Copyright

Notchin' Boots Series
These women own their sexuality and aren't ashamed of the notches on their bedposts. Will the heroes who come into their lives be enough to show them how good commitment can be and get these ladies to throw out their little black books? Join some of your favorite romance authors for the Notchin' Boots Series.

✿ Created with Vellum

Acknowledgments

Jessica, you are summer and I am winter. Always.

Danni, this journey is so crazy! Thank you for being here with me!

JD, thank you for spending late nights with and making sure I listened even when I didn't want to. Love you.

Nicole, I'm forever grateful that you're in my life.

Carissa, thank you for everything you do.

Arthur, you've always supported me no matter how crazy my ideas are. I love you so much.

Mom, you've always been my biggest supporter and I don't know where I'd be without you.

Caoimhe-Lea, you drive me absolutely fucking crazy. But I wouldn't have it any other way. Love you.

Taye, and everyone I'm forgetting who has supported my crazy ideas and continue to be with me, thank you. I truly couldn't do this without all of you.

Information

No part of this book or graphics were made with AI.
HUMAN CREATION ONLY

Notch the Plan has NO cheating with a guaranteed HEA. It is a standalone but is connected to my Cimaruta MC Chicago Series and my Mancini Legacy Series.

There are not a lot of dark moments or dark issues in my books, there still are the occasions that have to do with kidnapping, domestic abuse, and assault.

Check out my website for current news and trigger warnings.

Mancini Legacy and Cimaruta MC family trees.
Nataliearthurbooks.com

Mancini Legacy and Cimaruta MC Dictionary

Cage - Motorized vehicle with four wheels. (Cars)

Chicago Panthers - Professional baseball team.

Chicago Redhawks - Professional hockey team.

Cimaruta MC, Chicago - Chicago Motorcycle club, Mother charter

Cut - Vest that patched in members of the MC wear to identify who they are and their rank.

Lake Renegade Township - Town owned by the Mancini family.

Lucciola Island - 'Firefly' Island, owned by the Mancini family and located in Massachusetts.

Lucciola Memorial Hospital - Hospital in Lake Renegade Township.

Mancini Grill - 5-star restaurant located inside the Legacy Hotel.

Rockers - Top rocker has the club's name on it, the bottom rocker has the club's location.

Sprite Lake Village - Town in Illinois, owned by the Laurent family.

The Legacy Hotel - Hotel in downtown Chicago owned by the Mancini family.

Galway - Town in Ireland.

ITALIAN

Amore - Love.

Coglione - Asshole.

Colomba mia - My dove.

Cugino - Cousin.

Cuore mio - My heart.

Dolcezza - Sweetness.

Famiglia - Family.

Figlio - Son.

Fratello - Brother.

Il mio mondo - My world.

Il mio pinguino - My penguin.

Mai Andato - Never Gone.

Mi dispiace - I'm sorry.

Mi passerotta - My little sparrow.

Nonno - Grandfather.

Nonna - Grandmother.

Ti abbiamo aspettato - We waited for you.

Ti voglio bene - I love you.

Zio - Uncle.

Zia -Aunt.

IRISH

Aintín - Aunty

Is í Gàidhlig ár gcéad teanga - Gaelic is our first language.

M'anam - My soul

Mo stór - My treasure.

FRENCH

D'accord petite sœur - Okay little sister

Je t'aime et Lorenzo - I love you and Lorenzo

Je t'aime - I love you

Je vous aime tous les deux - I love you both

Princesse - Princess

Toujours - Always

Toujours mes frères - Always my brothers

Tu es ma princesse - You are my princess

Cimaruta MC

President - Giacomo 'Forza' Bastianini

Vice President - Celestino 'Giustizia' Bastianini

Sgt-At-Arms - Francesco 'Bestia' Bastianini

Treasurer - Luciana 'Fuoco' Bastianini

Secretary - Isabella 'Dolce' Bastianini

Historian - Caitríona 'Forte' Bastianini

Road Captain - Connor 'Azrael' Byrne

Chaplain - Brennan 'Raziel' Doyle

Enforcer - Liam 'Amante' Murphy

Enforcer - Valentino 'Ombra' Marconi

Enforcer - Romana 'Fantasma' Vietti

Enforcer - Mitchell 'Granchio' Harris

Enforcer - Hollis 'Cavallo' Taylor

Enforcer - Rónán 'Ghiaccio' O'Callaghan

Enforcer - Fintan 'Toro' O'Callaghan

Prospect - Anthony Grimes

FAUSTO & LUNA
GRANDPARENTS
GIACOMO
SON
CAITRÍONA
DAUGHTER IN LAW
CELESTINO
GRANDSON
FRANCESCO
GRANDSON
SAOIRSE
GREAT GRANDDAUGHTER
ISABELLA
GRANDDAUGHTER
LUCIANA
GRANDDAUGHTER
GRAYSON
GREAT GRANDSON
BASTIANINI
FAMILY

KEARNEY FAMILY

Liam & Orfhlaith
GRANDPARENTS

Caitríona
DAUGHTER

Giacomo
SON IN LAW

Celestino
GRANDSON

Francesco
GRANDSON

Saoirse
GREAT GRANDDAUGHTER

Isabella
GRANDDAUGHTER

Luciana
GRANDDAUGHTER

Grayson
GREAT GRANDSON

GIACOMO
CAITRÍONA
CELESTINO
ISABELLA
FRANCESCO
LUCIANA
MAEVE
RÓNÁN
SAOIRSE
GRAYSON
BASTIANINI
FAMILY

MANCINI FAMILY

Pietro & Alessia
Grandparents

Enea (T)
Son

Antonio (T)
Son

Leonardo (T)
Son

Gráinne
Daughter-in-law

Rosaura
Daughter-in-law

Sebastiano*
Grandson

Salvatore^
Grandson

Domenico*
Grandson

Fiorella^
Granddaughter

Lorenzo+
Grandson

Gianluca^
Grandson

Giovanna+
Granddaughter

Rowan
Great Grandson

(T) = Triplets
* = Twins
+ = Twins
^ = Triplets

MANCINI FAMILY

Antonio (T)

Enea (T)

Gráinne

Leonardo (T)

Rosaura

Sebastiano*

Salvatore^

Schuyler

Sansone

Fiorella^

Domenico*

Lorenzo+

Gianluca^

Giovanna+

Declan

Rowan

(T) = Triplets

* = Twins

+ = Twins

^ = Triplets

O'CALLAGHAN

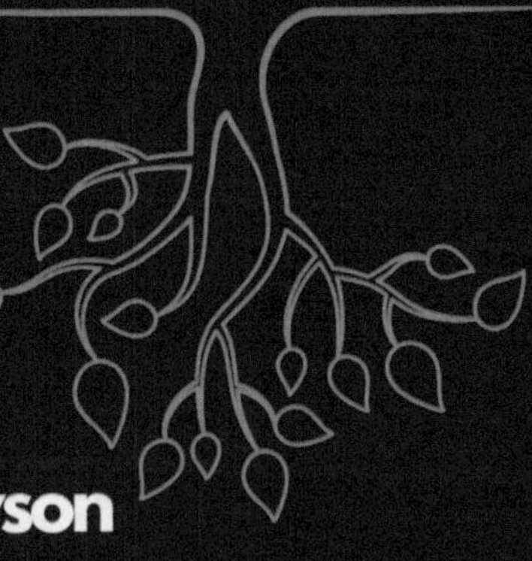

Contents

Notch The Plan

Chapter One

Liam

I always knew what path my life would take. I was named after my grandfather, Liam Murphy, who was one of the first prospects for the Cimaruta Motorcycle Club.

My da, Kieran Murphy, prospected the day he turned eighteen and after a few years, was promoted to chaplain of the MC. I started prospecting for the Cimaruta on my eighteenth birthday as well.

When I was sixteen, my da was killed in a fight between the Cimaruta and the Crimson Royals, a rival MC out of California. They ambushed some of our brothers at a bar we own called The Hawk's Nest. Fucking chickenshits. Those pussies threw Molotov cocktails into the bar and tried to run. Our guys got some shots off as soon as they got their heads clear. They got a few of them, one fatally. Every member of every MC wears a cut—a vest that identifies what club they belong to. Before the Royals could get their club's cut off the dead guy, they heard sirens approaching. So they scattered like cockroaches and left him there. There's still bad blood between our clubs to this day.

I grew up with our club president's kids and I'm two years older than the eldest set of Bastianini twins. When Isabella and Luciana—the younger twins—turned sixteen, Valentino 'Ombra' Marconi and I were selected to be their bodyguards. Ombra had already been a patched member for five years. I had only been a patched member for a few months, but because of my history with the family, they chose me to be Luciana's guard.

My parents were high school sweethearts. They got married the weekend after they graduated from high school and had me a year later. The day my da died, I watched the light go out in my mother, Kylie's, eyes. She held on for two more years until I turned eighteen. I could see how hard it was for her to do that, but she did it for me because she was worried I would end up in the foster care system or be left to fend for myself.

In the end, her love for my da, the sadness and pain of losing him, won. She took her life on what would've been their twentieth wedding anniversary. I was a little late coming home that night because I had stopped to get her some flowers. I found her lying on my da's side of their bed, clutching his pillow. At first I thought she was just sleeping, until I noticed she was wearing his club jacket that he had loved so much. She had chosen to take a bottle of pills and washed them down with a bottle of whiskey. I had thought she was finally getting better. We had spent the previous week doing things she and my da loved to do and things we had done as a family. Never in my wildest dreams did I think that would be the last week we'd have together. I miss them both every fucking day.

That night, I told myself I would never let anyone get close enough to make me feel the way my mam did about my da. What's the point of falling in love when you could lose that person with no warning? Fuck that. Keep it casual and no one gets hurt—I don't even take them out on dates. It's one night of fun, nothing more. And *never* more than one night.

Because I'm Luciana's bodyguard, I live with her and Rónán O'Callaghan, her fiancé. Both Luciana and Rónán's brothers dance for Magic Nights Chicago, which is owned by Celestino and Francesco Bastianini. They keep trying to get me to dance for the company. Fuck that. It's bad enough I have to be at Luminescence every weekend for the shows. I'm not about to get up there and take my clothes off.

Charmaine

Love is a lie. There's no such thing as true love or soulmates or love at first sight. There's only heartbreak and lies. My parents, Russell and Heather Holt, are the perfect example of that. They had my sister Violet when they were sixteen. Then a year later, my brother Nathan. They got married at eighteen, and had Trevor about a year after that. I came a year after Trevor. So by the time they were twenty one, they were married, with four kids under the age of five.

That's when I think things started to go bad. My parents had barely graduated high school, nevermind college. My mom worked as the head housekeeper for one of the biggest hotel chains in Chicago. My dad? Well, he tried all kinds of jobs, finally settling on bartending and becoming an apprentice in the Carpenters Union. It took him five years to become a journeyman carpenter. But he loves it and now has his own business making custom furniture.

I would say about thirteen years into their marriage was when the cheating started. My dad was, and still is, a very attractive man. I've seen firsthand how women throw themselves at him. And with him working at a bar—well, you can imagine how that can go. My mom met other men at the hotel where she worked. I know my parents started out loving each other. I have tons of memories of watching my parents hugging and kissing. But by the time I was ten years old, my parents spent more time away from than with each other. And when they were together, all they did was fight. When I was twelve, my mom got pregnant and my dad said it wasn't his. Turns out he was right. She had a miscarriage, but that was the end of their marriage. During that time, they never treated any of us badly. They truly loved us, they just didn't love each other anymore. I'm not sure why, but they stayed married until I turned eighteen. But I know that they slept in separate rooms and only interacted with one another when it came to us kids. At school functions and sporting events, people saw the perfect loving family. Their 'extracurricular' activities were discreet while we were in school. I asked them why they did that, and they both said it was because they didn't want us to have to deal with their choices. Society has a bad habit of casting dirty looks onto the kids when they have parents who do things like that. Like I said, they really loved us and made sure us kids had a good life.

Watching my parents together when I was younger, I was determined that I would find my person. The one man that would be my partner, my equal. One that I could depend on when I needed to, and I would do the same for him. Even if my parents couldn't make it work, there had to be someone out there for me. I was so happy when I met Rex; I thought he was the perfect man. Oh how wrong I was. Fuck love.

Chapter Two

Liam

My weekends are spent at Luminescence. Luciana is a photographer for the club along with one of her best friends, Owen Bayne. Her fiancé, Rónán, is a dancer for the club. The women that come to the shows are sometimes crazy but still a lot of fun. Although every once in a while we get one that makes my job harder. It's definitely not a job that allows me to have a lot of free time. But when I do get some time to myself, I usually head down to the bar the MC owns. All the single guys on the council usually hang out together.

We also invite the prospects, to get to know them better and to make sure they're going to fit in. Our prospects do the regular shit that's required of them on a day-to-day basis, but seeing how they act in a casual setting is just as important. We don't want members that can't be respectful to each other and to others outside the MC. That was a big deal to our founders—having the foundation of our club be family, blood and chosen. And having respect for others outside the club—unless they disrespect us first. Then you'll see how the *family* aspect works in our club.

Tonight is one of the rare nights that we have off from guard duty. Of course, the minute we sit down at the bar, women are coming over and asking us to buy them drinks. Some are hangers-on that are constantly at our bar and at the clubhouse. Their goal is to get one of the brothers to take them as his 'old lady'. That generally doesn't happen with these kinds of women. We also had to tell them not to walk around naked in the clubhouse. Having women on the council has made us look at the old ways and make some changes. But at the bars it's like a free-for-all.

Looking around, I notice a few new faces and holy shit, one of them is fucking gorgeous. A lot of the women who come here are looking for some fun. But that group of girls look like they're making their own fun.

"Hey Charlie, do you know who those women are at that table over there?" I ask our bartender.

"They came in about an hour ago, said it's girl's night out. Anyone in particular?" He smiles.

"Can you send them a round for me? Whatever they want. And yeah, I want to know what the brunette with the curls is drinking."

"Sure thing, boss."

"Hey, handsome. Need some company tonight?" one of our regulars asks as she runs a finger down my chest.

"Hey, Sylvie. Not tonight, sweetheart."

She pouts and slides her hand up my thigh. "Are you sure? You look like you need some—"

I stop her from finishing. "I'm good. Thanks."

She sighs and moves on to Fantasma, one of my club brothers, who gives her a smile but tells her no as well.

I can't take my eyes off my mystery woman, and when Charlie takes the drinks over, he points to me. I raise my beer and smile at them. They all smile back and wave, but there's only one I'm really looking at. And I think she's finally noticing me, too.

As I'm watching her, a guy struts up to them and puts his arm around her shoulders. The look on her face is telling me that she's not into it. In fact, she looks a little scared, and I don't like that one fucking bit. All the women at the table look like they don't want him there. I stand up and make my way over to them.

Charmaine

Tonight is a rare girl's night out with my besties and my sister. We try to do this at least once a month. Work and life always seem to get in the way, but we still try.

The bartender comes over to our table with a round of drinks.

"This is from Amante. He's the biggest one at the bar." He chuckles as we all turn our heads to look.

What we see is a sexy-as-hell biker raising his beer at us. Holy crap. I'd like to have him for one night. The look on his face is saying he'd like to show at least one of us a good time. He's huge.

The t-shirt he's wearing is barely hanging on, his muscles are fighting it from all directions. And his tats. Yum. I'd like to lick those tats...maybe they'll taste like ice cream?

"Hey baby, I didn't know you were coming out tonight." A voice I never wanted to hear again pulls me out of my ice cream fantasy.

The looks on my friends' faces says it all.

"What are you doing here, Rex?" It's taking everything in me to keep my voice even.

"I was driving by and decided to get a drink. It's just fate that you're here too."

"Are you following me?" I snap at him.

"I told you. I was just driving by and—" he starts to say when Violet cuts him off.

"You're not welcome here," she says. "Get the fuck away from my sister," she growls at him. Rex is one man no one will ever forgive. And at this point, anger is the only emotion I have left for him.

Rex laughs. "You always were a bitch, Vi."

"Don't talk to my sister like that. You need to leave. The restraining order is specific, and you're within one hundred feet of my personal bubble."

"Fuck your restraining order and what the fuck is your 'personal bubble'? You really think that piece of paper will keep me away from you?" he hisses in my ear.

"You should listen to the ladies. Get your hands off her and get the fuck out," a deep voice says.

Rex turns toward it and is forced to look up.

"Who the fuck do you think you are?" he says, but his voice shakes like a scared little boy.

"I'm the one who's going to kick your ass if you don't get out of my bar. Now."

"Fuck you and fuck your bar. Let's go, Charmaine."

"Did you not hear her say 'restraining order'? I believe that means you're leaving alone," the mystery man says to Rex.

We watch him gesture to the guys he was sitting with at the bar.

"Prospect, 86 this asshole."

"Sure thing, Amante," the one he called 'prospect' says. "Let's go."

"Don't touch me. You can't force me out of a public place."

"Actually, we can. This bar is owned by the Cimaruta MC, and it's a private establishment," the sexy giant says calmly. I haven't heard him raise his voice yet—he's so huge I don't think he has to very often. Rex is six feet even, and this guy has like five inches on him and at least fifty pounds of lickable, tattooed muscle.

We all watch the prospect half-drag Rex out of the bar. He's making such a scene—screaming and carrying on that he's being treated unfairly and that he's going to call the cops. I look at the hunky man standing next to me and he's smiling. I think he's enjoying this.

"Thank you for that," Violet says.

"My pleasure. If anyone bothers you again, just tell the guy at the door or the bartender. They'll always have your back."

"I'm Violet. This is my sister Charmaine, and our friends, Chloe, Faith and Lila."

"Nice to meet you, I'm Amante."

"That's an unusual name," Chloe says, smiling.

My hunky tattooed man smiles at Chloe. Which makes me frown slightly. Why? I have no idea. While I'm trying to figure out why it bothers me so much, my sister elbows me in the side.

"What's with the frown?" she whispers.

"I'm not," I argue quietly.

She rolls her eyes at me. "Do you like Muscle Man? Because I think he likes you. He may be talking to Chloe, but he's definitely watching you."

"No he's not. Besides, I don't want him."

"You always were a shitty liar." She laughs at me. Times like these, I think about how it would be nice to be an only child.

"I'm going to disown you if you don't shut up," I threaten her.

She starts cackling. Like the wicked witch in the Wizard of Oz. And because she's making a ton of noise, Amante is now looking at us. Damn loud mouth.

"Can I get you ladies another round?" he asks while staring at me.

"We should probably be buying you and your friends a round instead. Would you guys like to join us?" Chloe asks.

"Drinks are on me. But if you want, I'll invite my brothers over."

"Yes, please," Chloe, Lila and Faith say together. I'm sure Violet would join in, but she's still busy cackling. I'm tempted to push her off her chair.

I watch Amante walk back over to the guys he called his brothers. After a few minutes, the whole group heads our way, carrying extra drinks. They pull another table over to connect with ours.

"Faith, Lila, Chloe, Violet and Charmaine, these are my brothers—Giustizia, Ombra, Cavallo and Granchio."

"You have interesting names." Lila chuckles.

"Road names, darling." Cavallo smiles at Lila as he sits next to her.

"So wait, you have another name?" She scoots closer to him.

"Of course. My mother would never name me 'Cavallo' on purpose."

Lila laughs. "Okay, what's your real name? And what does 'Cavallo' mean?"

Cavallo sighs. "Hollis," he says softly, but not soft enough because Granchio snorts.

"What's wrong with 'Hollis'?" Lila snaps at Granchio. "I think that's a great name."

"Cavallo means 'horse' in Italian," Cavallo explains to her.

"Can I call you 'Hollis'?" she asks him. "And why do you have the name 'Cavallo'?"

"Sweetheart, you can call me whatever you want," he says, smiling. "We all get road names when we become members of our club. I got 'Cavallo' because my president said I was a workhorse when I was a prospect."

"Well that makes sense, but I still like 'Hollis' better," she smiles back at him.

I've never really seen Lila interested in anyone. Usually she's content just drooling over men. All the Cimaruta men are delicious, but only one makes me want to consider dating again.

"What does 'Amante' mean?" I ask as he sits down next to me.

Chapter Three

Liam

I can see the pride on Hollis' face when Lila defends him. He once made the mistake of telling the brothers how much he hates his name. So of course, they've given him shit about it ever since. Because that's what we do.

I pull up a chair to sit next to Charmaine. I'm still not sure what is drawing me to her, but I need to be near her.

"Amante means 'lover'," I say to her.

"So since Cavallo got his name because of his work ethic, does that mean you're a player?"

The look on her face is killing me. "No.

When I was little, my mam always said I'd grow up to be a lady killer. I didn't quite understand what she meant, so one day I told her I wanted to be a lover, not a fighter. When it was time for me to get my road name, my president remembered my mam telling that story," I explain to her.

She smiles that smile that I've come to like—maybe too much—in this short time.

"I love that," she says.

"Can I ask who that asshole was?" I whisper to her.

She sighs softly. "He's my crazy, abusive, shitbag ex. Thank you for kicking him out."

I nod as I look into her clear blue eyes. "You'll always be safe here. My club owns this bar and we don't stand for assholes. Ever."

"You mean the Cimaruta MC? I've seen people with vests like the one you have on around the city. That's your club?"

"Well, I'm part of it. Giustizia over there is the VP. I'm an enforcer."

She looks over at Giustizia, and I expect her to go all gaga over him like most women do. But to my surprise, she immediately swings her gaze back to me.

"What's an enforcer?" she asks.

"I make sure that people are respecting my

club brothers and sisters. If anyone causes problems, I take care of it."

"So you're like a protector. You protect your family."

"I do. I protect the ones I care about."

She gives me a big smile. "I like that."

I've never met a woman that made me want to get to know her. Usually when I'm with a woman, it's just superficial attraction. But this beauty makes me actually want to know the real her, not just spend the night together. What the fuck is going on? What's wrong with me?

"Are you and your friends celebrating something tonight?"

"No, just girl's night out."

"I'm glad you chose the Hawk's Nest for it."

Her smile lights up her face, and it makes me smile.

"Me too. Actually, it was Lila's idea. Last Friday, she went with Faith, Chloe and Violet to an all-male show. She heard that some of the dancers hang out here." She chuckles. "So the four of them wanted to come and see if they could meet them."

I laugh. "At Luminescence?"

"How did you know?"

"I know the guys who dance there. Giustizia over there is one of them."

"No wonder Faith keeps staring at him."

"You didn't go to the show?" I ask.

"No, I wasn't feeling well, so I stayed home. But they want to go again this weekend, so I'll probably be going this time."

I involuntarily growl softly. I don't want her drooling over the dancers. I don't care that I know all of them and they're all my brothers. If they touch her, I'll have to kick their asses and that won't go over too well. Wait. What the fuck?

"I can get you all VIP tickets if you want."

"What's the difference?" she asks.

"Regular admission gets you a seat in rows three to ten and general access after the show. VIP gets you a booth, table or a seat in the first two rows, and you'll have a chance to be one of the girls picked to go up on stage. You also have access to the VIP section, which means you get to hang out with the dancers after the show, plus free drinks."

"Wow. You really do know what goes on there," she teases.

I chuckle. "Well, I told you I know the dancers and I also work security for them. So I'm there every show."

"Do you, um...enjoy the shows?"

My eyes get bigger. "Are you asking me if I'm gay?"

"Um I-I guess I am?" she stutters out.

I take her hand and kiss it, then lean in, brushing my lips against her ear. "No, amore. I'm not gay," I whisper.

She visibly shivers as she pulls back slightly and looks at me, slowly smiling.

"Are all the dancers married or taken? Are any single?"

I frown slightly. "I can introduce you to the single ones, if that's what you want."

"Not for me. I was thinking for my besties," she says as she keeps her hold on my hand.

Thank God. I didn't want to have to fight any of my brothers tonight because my girl was lusting after one of them. Wait a fucking minute. My girl? Where the fuck did that come from? Maybe I'm sick. That has to be it, I caught a cold, and it's affecting my brain. It's really the only sane explanation.

We spend the night laughing and listening to the girls tell stories about their lives. I can see the sister bond between Charmaine and Violet is very strong. In fact, all the girls are super close. Towards the end of the night, they all decide it's time to do shots. I decline—I really don't enjoy drinking till I'm drunk. I like a little buzz, nothing more. Even less if I'm riding or driving, it's never worth the risk.

Charmaine

Who knew girl's night out at a biker bar could be so much fun? Not me, that's for sure. And to think I almost said no to coming out tonight. That guy Cavallo hasn't left Lila's side since they all joined us. And she doesn't seem to mind. I enjoy seeing my friends happy and Lila deserves to be happy. I wish Vi would find someone; she hasn't had a solid relationship for a few years now. It looks like Granchio's into her and she keeps flirting with him, so that's something new.

Rex was my first love. I gave him everything because I thought he was someone special. Then I found out what he was really like. He's a lying, cheating bastard and I didn't see it for two years. In fact, I think he was always like that, I just had blinders on when it came to him. He conned me with his looks and his charm—I believed everything he said. The business trips, the late nights at work...yeah. Idiot. When I found out, I left him and he's been stalking me ever since.

It's been almost a year now, but he still shows up wherever I am and tries to act like nothing's changed. Even when I see him out with other women, he'll make it a point to come over to me. I feel sorry for the women who date Rex. He thinks he's the perfect man and everyone else is inferior—especially women. Then there's the phone calls and texts. I had to change my number twice now, and somehow he's gotten it again.

When Amante stood up for me tonight, it made me feel safe. For the first time since I left him, I felt like Rex couldn't touch me. But I worry about when it's time to leave, and tomorrow, and the day after that. Will he show up and try to hurt me again? My gut is saying yes. The worst part is Amante won't be around to protect me.

"Time for shots!" Faith cheers.

Everyone laughs. "What kind of shots do you want?" I ask.

"LEMON DROPS!" Chloe yells.

Amante gets up laughing and goes to order our shots. "Another round of drinks too?" he asks before walking too far away.

"YES PLEASE!" Chloe yells more.

"I think Chlo is about done." Violet chuckles.

"I am not." Chloe pouts. "I'm just having a good time."

Amante comes back with the shots and drinks.

"Are you not drinking?" I ask him.

"I don't like to be drunk or buzzed when I ride my bike," he explains.

Holy hell. He's sexy as sin *and* responsible? I could only wish for a man like him. Protective, too. When I dreamt about my perfect man, it was always about how protective he was of me and our family. Amante sounds like family is the most important thing to him. So even if he wasn't panty-dropping gorgeous, I would still want to know him.

"That's why we took a cab tonight. None of us wanted to be the designated driver." I chuckle.

"Don't worry, we'll make sure you all get home safe."

"Yeah, but who's home will you be taking Charmy to?" Vi cackles. Yep. Time for a new sister. I glare at her, which makes her cackle more.

Amante chuckles. "I'll take her anywhere she wants to go."

Holy shit my face feels like it's on fire. I can't even look at him—if I do, he'll know what I'm thinking. Because I'm pretty sure it's written all over my face.

"You better take care of her," Vi says, suddenly serious. "My sister is a good person, and she deserves only the best."

Amante nods at Vi, then takes my hand and kisses it.

"I promise," he says as he looks deep into my eyes. Staring back at him, I get lost in his beautiful gray eyes. It's like looking into a storm that's threatening to sweep me away.

"Earth to Charmy!" Chloe yells.

Was I ignoring them? Shit.

"Huh? Why are you yelling, Chlo?" I ask.

"Because you weren't listening to us. We were talking to you, but you and Amante here just kept staring into each other's eyes. Like puppy dogs, you know, like *Lady and the Tramp*." Chloe giggles.

"Wait, are you calling me a tramp?" Amante gasps, his eyes twinkling like he wants to laugh.

Chloe scrunches up her face. "You know, I didn't really think about it. I guess you can be Lady."

"Wait, that means you're saying I'm the Tramp." I blink at her.

Chloe looks back and forth between Amante and me with her mouth flapping open like a fish trying to breathe out of water.

Everyone busts out laughing. I love my girls.

Chapter Four

Charmaine

I wake up feeling like I got run over by a truck. And I smell like a brewery. Holy fuck, I'm sweating. Did I turn the heat on before I fell into bed? Wait. These sheets don't feel like mine and there's someone in the bathroom because I just heard the shower turn on. I pry my eyes open and look around. It's a hotel room. What the fuck did I do last night? I need to get out of here before whoever's in that bathroom comes out.

I'm not naked, so that's good...I think. I get out of bed and see my jeans and jacket folded neatly on a chair, along with my purse. Trying not to make too much noise, I get my jeans on, then grab my jacket and purse. I check quickly for my phone and keys. All there. I get out of the room as fast as I can.

Getting into the elevator, I cringe at my reflection. I look like roadkill. And feel like it too. I keep trying to remember what happened last night, but after those two rounds of shots, everything gets fuzzy. I do remember all of us sitting with the hot bikers. And Amante. My god, he was hot, but I doubt I'll see him again. Even though I really want to. I need to get home and shower, then call Vi. Maybe she remembers more than me. I can't even remember the last time I drank this much.

I get on my phone and order a rideshare. Right as I get in, my phone starts ringing. I see my sister's face on the screen. I decide to text her instead; I hate talking on the phone in rideshares, you know they're listening.

Charmaine: Hey sis. I'm in a rideshare. I'll call you when I get home

Violet: Okay. How long? I think I'm dying

Charmaine: Maybe thirty minutes. But I wanna shower first. Dying=hungover?

Violet: Mm-hmm. Why didn't you shower with your muscley man before you left? I think I'm gonna puke (vomit emoji)

Charmaine: Gross. I didn't need to know that

She's not talking about Amante, is she? Is that who was in the bathroom?

Charmaine: I don't know what you're talking about

Violet: Oh shit. Was he that bad in bed?? A man that sexy can't be

Charmaine: I'll call you after I shower. Now shush

Violet: (vomit emoji)

I can just imagine my sister laughing on her end. But what did she mean about my 'muscley man'? Shit. Did I fuck Amante last night? For the first time since breaking up with Rex, I met someone I really wanted to get to know. But now I think I might have screwed that up. Not only did I sleep with him, I snuck out without saying anything. He probably thinks I'm crazy and doesn't want anything to do with me. I'm such an idiot.

Liam

When I got out of the shower, she was gone. I should be happy about that—mornings after are always so sticky. You have to act like you're going to call them, when you know you won't. But this time I don't feel relieved. There's a sick feeling in my stomach that I don't like. It's saying I may have lost someone worth keeping.

Meeting Charmaine last night changed something in me. I've listened to Luciana talk about how it felt when she met Rónán. But I always figured it was a freak thing that only happened to her. That kind of instant attraction doesn't happen to the rest of us. But after last night...it might have happened to me because I can't stop thinking about her. Her smile, her face, the curves I want to run my hands all over. I don't want her to think she's just a passing sex toy. Like an idiot, I didn't get her damn number. What makes it worse is that she snuck out while I was in the shower. Maybe she doesn't feel the same way I do. When did I turn into the sappy person standing here?

I sigh and head back home. I need to get her out of my system and our morning session is the perfect way to do that. Ombra, Fantasma and I work out together every day—along with the Bastianinis and O'Callaghans.

No matter how much I try to stop thinking about Charmaine, I just can't seem to do it. I'm so fucked.

"Are you okay?" Luciana asks while spotting for me.

"I'm fine. Why?"

"You seem distracted. You're never distracted."

"Not distracted, just a little tired."

"Charmaine keep you up all night?" Ombra teases.

"Ohhhhh it's a girl that's got you like this." Luciana snickers. I can see the rest of them starting to pay attention to our conversation. Bunch of nosy shits.

I glare at both of them. "There is no girl."

Ombra snorts. Actually snorts. What the fuck?

"No girl, huh? I was there last night. I mean, if you can't remember, I can call the prospect to refresh your memory. Oh, and Giustizia can help with that too."

Luciana claps her hands and giggles like Saoirse, Francesco's four-year-old daughter, does when she's excited. I glare at her.

"Yes, please!" she says to Ombra while laughing her ass off.

"Aren't we here to work out? You're all acting like kids," I growl.

Great. Now everyone is laughing and looking at me. Times like these make me start to rethink this whole 'family' thing.

"It's okay, Amante, we know what it's like to fall in love," Isabella, Luciana's twin, says sweetly. Way too sweetly. I roll my eyes at her.

"I'm not in love."

"You're blushing. Holy shit! You're lying!" Isabella shouts at me.

"Why are you yelling? I'm right in front of you and I'm not deaf." I blink at her.

"Was I? Sorry. But don't change the subject. Tell us who she is."

I can see they're not going to let this go. Now, some of them are just sitting on the equipment, waiting for me to tell the story. There's really no story to tell, all I know is her name and that I want to know more about her. But as for story time? I got nothing.

"Fine, I met a woman last night. But nothing happened, she was with her friends and we all hung out with them at the Hawk's Nest."

"Bullshit. You left together and you didn't come home till this morning." Giustizia laughs.

"Yeah, she left with me, but she was so drunk I wasn't about to touch her."

"Always the gentleman." Luciana smiles.

No matter how much shit Luciana dishes out to me, she always has my back too.

"I will admit I want to know her better," I say.

"So call her, maybe invite her to come and work out with us? Less pressure that way," she suggests.

"I would, but I'm an idiot and didn't get her number."

Some of the guys snicker.

"Shut it," Luciana snaps at them. "We'll find her. One of them had to pay the bill last night, right?"

"I think they paid for their first round of drinks, but I got the rest."

"Well, let's ask Charlie if they paid with a card. We can get the name and go from there."

I laugh at Luciana; she sounds so excited to track Charmaine down.

"Her name is Charmaine, but her friends were calling her Charmy."

"That's cute. What else can you tell me? Did she say where she works? Or what she does for work?"

I laugh more. "Her sister's name is Violet and all the girls that were there work with her. But I didn't ask what she did. Cavallo was talking to her friend, Lila. Maybe he has some info."

Luciana marches over to Cavallo and starts interrogating him. The rest of us can't help but laugh as we get back to our workout.

"Holy shit, Fuoco is terrifying. She was grilling me like I stole something!" Cavallo blurts out to me.

"She's a firecracker. You should know that by now." I snicker.

"Yeah, well, I've never been on that side of one of her interrogations."

He looks a little traumatized, which makes me laugh more.

"Did you give her what she wanted?" I ask.

"Of course I did...well the info I had, anyway. I didn't have enough for her, though. Because she said men are worthless at intel."

"That's my sister for you." Bestia laughs. When we're all together with our club brothers and sisters, we use our road names. Sometimes, in more casual settings, we'll use our first names. But for the most part, it's road names all the way.

Chapter Five

Charmaine

I need to stop obsessing over Amante. Since the minute he sent those drinks over last night, he's all I've been thinking about. Now that I know it was probably him that I walked out on, I feel so stupid. I didn't even get his number, because like a dumbass, I forgot to ask. At least I know where he hangs out. Maybe I can accidentally-on-purpose bump into him again this week. He told me that he doesn't get out a lot, though. Which I get, because with the amount I work, I really only get one day off. I realize now that while I didn't ask him what he did for work, he did say he's an enforcer for the MC and he does security at Luminescence. I'm guessing those are his jobs?

Lila spent the night talking to the guy they called Cavallo. She refused to call him that, which made me chuckle. His real name is Hollis. I kept switching back and forth with Amante, whose real name is Liam. I like both his names, they suit him well.

I'm the manager at the Mancini Grill—it's the restaurant inside the Legacy Hotel that's owned by the Mancini Family. They're a very well-known family here in Chicago. They own several clubs and stores, as well as the hotel. I've been there for four years now. I started as a busser, then moved on to waiting tables. When one of our bartenders left, I asked if I could have that job. Eventually they offered me the opportunity to manage the entire restaurant. It's been a lot of fun working there, and I can't imagine working for any other company. The Mancinis make sure that every employee is taken care of. Most restaurants don't offer sick pay or medical, dental and vision. But the Mancinis do. Everyone that works at least twenty hours a week gets those benefits. And if you're a full-time employee that puts in forty hours a week? You get two weeks of paid vacation per year and a 401k.

Back to my daydreaming about Amante. Maybe I'll go back to the Hawk's Nest and see if they'll tell me anything about him. I should text Lila too, she and Cavallo hit it off last night. She had to have been smarter than me and gotten his number, right?

Walking into my apartment, I sigh. I need to shower. I can smell myself and that's never a good thing. I suddenly feel sorry for the other people in the rideshare. They must think I'm an alcoholic or something. If it was Amante in that hotel bathroom, I'm kind of glad I ran away, considering the way I smell.

I text Lila as I get ready to shower. My crappy sister can wait.

> Charmaine: Hey! Did you by chance get Cavallo's number?

> Lila: Are you trying to steal my Hollis?

I snort.

> Charmaine: Not even. LOL. I was an idiot, and I didn't get Amante's number last night

> Lila: You want me to get his number for you? Hollis just left the hotel room, and I have a couple of hours before check out, so I got time. (cheesy smile emoji) He's meeting the guys at the gym. He asked if I wanted to go. HAHA. Wait, didn't you leave with Amante last night? Where are you?

Fuck. I don't want to admit I panicked and ran away cause I couldn't remember.

> Lila: Well?

Dammit. I think about what to say to Lila. If I lie, she'll find out anyway, so I might as well just admit I'm dumb.

> Charmaine: I'm an idiot. I woke up this morning in a hotel and couldn't remember what happened. I heard someone in the shower, so I snuck out

> Lila: What the fuck? Did you drink that much? Did he force himself on you?

Charmaine: Calm down. I don't think anything happened. I still had some clothes on when I woke up. Also, I don't think Amante is the type to force anyone

Lila: Hollis said Amante would never take advantage of a woman. So did you want Amante's number? He's with him now

Charmaine: Yes, please. I hope he says yes

Lila: We both think he will, but Hollis said he can't just give it to you without asking

Charmaine: Oh for sure, I don't mind. I'm just scared he'll say no. (sad face emoji) Wait, you know what? Give him my number instead. Tell him to text me if he wants

Lila: Are you sure?

Charmaine: Yes. Thank you (red heart emoji)

Lila: I got you, babe. Hollis said he gave it to him

I figure if he has my number and wants to see me again—even after I snuck out—he can text me.

There's a sick feeling in my stomach, though. What if he doesn't want to talk to me? I'm so stupid. And just like that, as I'm feeling sorry for myself, a text comes in.

Liam

"You're grumpy," Luciana says to me as we're finishing up our workout.

"I'm not grumpy." I frown. Shit, I am being grumpy, I still can't figure out how to find Charmaine. And it's all I can think about.

"Hey Amante, Lila said she was texting with Charmaine. First, Charmaine wanted your number. But then she said to give you hers," Cavallo says as he comes over to us.

Someone is smiling down on me today. I found my girl.

"So she wants me to text her?" I ask.

"Yep. Here's her number."

Cavallo rattles off Charmaine's number and I add it to my phone.

> Amante: Hey, beautiful. Are you okay? When I got out of the shower, you were gone

I put my phone down and try to engage with my club family. But it's really hard to do while I'm waiting for her to respond.

> Charmaine: Hi. I'm so sorry I snuck out. You must think I'm a crazy person

> Amante: Not even a little. Are you okay? I hope I didn't scare you off

Holy shit, I sound like I'm begging her to tell me we're okay. What in the actual fuck?

> Charmaine: I'm good. I'm a little hungover though. How are you doing?

> Amante: I'm great. We're at the gym if you wanna come work out

> Charmaine: Thanks but no, I don't think my body would appreciate that (laughing emoji)

> Amante: LOL

> Charmaine: So I feel dumb asking this, but what happened last night? The last thing I remember is drinking at the bar

> Amante: You don't remember anything after that?

Charmaine: No. That's only happened to me once before, I feel so stupid

Amante: Don't feel stupid. I'm glad I was with you, we got a room at the Legacy Hotel and slept. You didn't seem super drunk but you were starting to pass out. Kissing was as far as we got

Charmaine: Thank you so much

Amante: Of course. Like I said, I'm glad it was me. I would hate for something to have happened to you. And I forgot to ask you last night, where do you work?

Charmaine: Mancini Grill, I'm the manager there. What do you do?

Amante: That's awesome! I know the Mancinis, they're a great family. Me? I'm a bodyguard

Charmaine: I love my job, the Mancinis take good care of us. Do you like being a bodyguard?

Amante: I do. It's with my club

Charmaine: That's awesome. Is that why you said you don't get much time off?

Amante: Yeah, I'm on duty almost 24/7. I hate to cut this short, but we're heading out right now. Can I text you later?

Charmaine: Definitely. You can text me anytime. Please drive safe (car emoji)

Amante: Always

While I was grumpy earlier, now I can't stop smiling. I found my girl. Now to make sure she knows it. How the fuck do I do that?

Chapter Six

Charmaine

After last night, I'm thrilled to be off work today. I don't think I could do it. No more drinking shots. Chloe loves her shots and I can guarantee she's just fine today. Not me, though. I can almost see the alcohol coming out of my pores. I seriously need to shower. My phone pings in my sister's text tone. Crap. I got so wrapped up talking to Amante that I forgot to text my sister.

Violet: DID YOU FORGET TO CALL ME? OR HELL AT LEAST TEXT?

Oh shit. I got the all caps from Vi.

Charmaine: Sorry, Vi. Just getting in the shower. Give me a few

Violet: (bored emoji) hurry up

I laugh at her text as I step into the tub.

Okay, at least I got rid of most of the alcohol smell. I still look like roadkill, though. But brushing my teeth makes me feel better.

Charmaine: Sorry, sis. Are you feeling okay?

Violet: Define okay. I feel like I was trampled by a herd of elephants. But I'm not throwing up…so I guess that's good?

Charmaine: LOL. Me too. We always say we won't do shots with Chlo and we do it anyway. Whyyyy

Violet: Cause we're stoooopid. LOL. Want me to come over and bring some food?

Charmaine: That sounds good. I don't wanna cook or go out in public again. I look like crap. Shots are definitely not my friend

Violet: Okay, I'll be there in like thirty minutes. Then you can tell me all about your muscley man

Charmaine: (eyeroll emoji) Drive safe. Love you

Violet: LOL. Love you too

Sitting alone, Amante keeps popping into my head. We're all supposed to go to the Magic Nights Chicago show on Friday. I open the group text I have with my girls to let them know Amante said he would get us VIP tickets.

Charmaine: Hey! So the show on Friday, we still going?

Lila: Duh

Chloe: Of course. You missed out on the last one

Charmaine: Pretty sure Vi's going too. She's on her way over right now. Amante told me last night he can get us VIP tickets if we want

Lila: Ohhh. I was going to get VIP last time but I didn't know if it'd be worth it. But it looked fun in the VIP section. Let's do it! Even if he can't get us tickets for some reason, it's not too bad. The regular one was $50 and I think the VIP is only like $75

Faith: Sounds good to me. I don't mind paying that if he can't get them for some reason

Charmaine: Sounds good. I'll ask him when I talk to him later

Chloe: Spill. We all know you left with him. And you, Lila, spill it about Horsey

Lila: OMG. He's not a horsey. Well, he's hung like one…and I may ridden him like one too… (horse and eggplant emoji)

Charmaine: Oh, ew. I really didn't need that visual

Lila: LOL. What's the matter? Is Amante not doing it for you? (shocked emoji)

Charmaine: Nothing happened. He said I was passing out, and he didn't want to take advantage of me

Chloe: He really is your Prince Charming. That's so awesome, Charmy

Lila: I agree

Charmaine: Okay, I think you're both hungover and delirious. I'm not starting anything serious with him. Remember Rex? Yeah, never again

Violet: Fuck that. Rex was a fucktard and you will not let him dictate the rest of your life

Charmaine: Stop texting and driving, Vi

Violet: I'm not, I'm getting our food. Stop changing the subject

Lila: Listen to your elders. Fuck Rex

Chloe: YES. FUCK REX

Faith: Rex can suck it

Charmaine: Psh. Elders. And no, relationships are bad. I swore I wouldn't be doing that again and not even Amante will change my mind

Violet: ...

Chloe: (eyeroll emoji)

Lila: SIGH

Chloe: We're coming over too.
Please buy enough for all of us, Vi

Violet: On it

No one will ever get me to change my mind about being in a relationship. Rex broke me in ways not even my sister knows about. And that's how it'll stay. I know this pull I feel towards Amante isn't like anything I've ever felt before. But when he finds out how broken I am? He'll go running, I just know it.

Even so, I can't help but think about him and what a life with him would be like. To be protected by him, that's what I thought I had with Rex. If only I had met Amante first. If only.

Liam

I want to see Charmaine tonight, but I don't know if that's being pushy. I mean, fuck, I've never wanted to see anyone again after just one night. And we didn't even do anything. I don't know how to do this, the only relationships I've had were with my parents and my MC family. The only thing I'm sure of is that I want Charmaine in my life, and I feel the need to protect her. I'm still not sure why. But I know I don't want anything bad to happen to her.

"You realize you haven't stopped smiling since you texted Charmaine earlier," Luciana says to me, smirking.

"She's something special. But I don't know how to do this."

"Do what?"

"Relationships. I've never had one."

"Is it because of me? I mean, because you have to be with me all the time?" she asks with a tinge of sadness.

"No. This isn't about you, Luciana. I love being able to watch over you. I've never had a relationship because I don't want to fall in love with someone, only to lose them—like my parents."

The whole club knows about what happened to my mam after we lost my da. But I always try to downplay it. I don't want anyone feeling sorry for me.

Luciana hugs me tight. "You're going to make the right woman very happy. And if it's

Charmaine? Then she'll be welcomed into our family with open arms."

Dammit. Leave it to Luciana to make me feel things. The Bastianini kids are the siblings I always wanted but never had. But Luciana holds a special place in my heart and not just because I'm her guard. She was kidnapped earlier this year, and it was the worst time for all of us. I felt like I failed her and our family.

It's part of the reason I don't go out much. I'm paranoid that something will happen while I'm gone. Not that Rónán and his brothers can't protect her, but it's my job. And they're my family.

I can't wait to introduce Charmaine to them.

Amante: Hey Charmaine, I put all of your names down for the VIP tickets. I did Friday and Saturday because I didn't know which night you wanted. Or if you wanted to do both

Charmaine: Thank you! Are the shows only Friday and Saturday?

Amante: Yes, only those two nights. Sometimes they do special shows, but for the most part, it's just those two

Charmaine: The girls are going to be so excited. Thank you again!

Amante: No problem, anything I can do for you, don't hesitate to ask

Charmaine: Will you be there?

Amante: Yes. I have no say in whether or not I'm there. I'm always there

Charmaine: LOL. From what Lila said, it's an awesome show

Amante: Sure, if you like half-naked men dancing around, it's AWESOME. Unfortunately, it's not something I enjoy. LOL

Charmaine: Aww. It sounds like fun, though…(tongue emoji)

Amante: LOL

I'm hoping to persuade everyone to go to the Grill to have dinner sometime this week. That way I can see my girl without being obvious about it. Fuck me, I really need to stop calling her my girl. I'm going to end up calling her that in front of her face.

Chapter Seven

Liam

Friday is here and we never made it to the Grill. Life has a way of putting the best plans on hold.

Charmaine and I have been texting every day. I feel like she's holding back even more than I am. I'm guessing her ex has something to do with that. If I find out he's hurt her more than just 'I don't love you, I'm done', he's a dead man.

Someone is threatening our club and we're in the process of finding out who it is. Usually it's another club flexing it's muscles, trying to intimidate us. Then there are times that it gets more serious and violent. That doesn't happen very often, but this threat is serious enough for Forza to impose the rule of 'no one goes anywhere alone'. Which tells us that he thinks it's a serious threat.

We've been pretty low key ever since our president, Forza, decided to take the club legit about seven years ago. We pay taxes and own businesses. Not everyone is happy with the changes, but so far most of the chapter clubs respect the decision and have begun to follow our lead. Times change and so we have to change too.

After texting with Charmaine, I do a sweep of the club with Ombra. We make sure all the cameras are up and running and that the security doors are locked and secure. We also have to verify that there's someone watching every entrance and exit. We installed cameras after Francesco was attacked in the club. At that time, we didn't have any video surveillance. It would've been different if we had it in place. But we can't look back, we have it now and it's helped us make sure not only our dancers are safe, but our customers too.

When she texts that they're on their way, I start feeling nervous. What the hell is going on? I don't get nervous. This is making me crazy. *She's* making me crazy.

Charmaine

The more I talk to Amante, the more the walls I constructed to keep everyone out are starting to crumble. I'm not sure how to feel about that. On one hand, he makes my heart flutter and I can't stop smiling. But on the other hand, I'm afraid of putting myself out there and getting hurt. Rex is back to stalking and harassing me. He makes comments about teaching Amante a lesson for throwing him out of the Hawk's Nest that night. And how if I think I'm going to be with someone like him, I better think twice. I haven't told Amante any of this. It's not really his problem to deal with, it's mine.

Tonight. Tonight is the night I've been waiting for. Not because I want to see the show, but because I get to see my Amante. Ugh, where did that come from? My Amante. He's not mine. Do I want him to be? A week ago, I would have said FUCK NO. But now? I don't know. Maybe.

We were all supposed to go together, but Lila backed out at the last minute. I have a feeling she's avoiding Hollis. That's something Lila and I have in common—we're both wary of putting ourselves out there again.

I told Amante I would text him when we're on our way. We decided to take a taxi in case we all want to drink. I'm so nervous and I can't explain why.

> Charmaine: Hey! We're going to be leaving soon. Is it too early?

> Amante: You'll probably get here right when we open. We start letting people in at five. Cavallo is on the door tonight

> Charmaine: Lila's not coming, though (sad face emoji)

> Amante: Cavallo's going to be disappointed. He can't stop talking about her. It's going to be a fun night. I made sure you got the front booth. It's more comfortable than the chairs

> Charmaine: Thank you so much for everything

> Amante: I told you anything you need, I'll do for you

I want to believe him so much, he's everything I've wanted in a man. And not just because of the way he looks. It's him. His love for the people closest to him. The outside screams mean, tough biker, but the inside says lover, brother, son, friend.

This club is amazing, the description that Lila gave me doesn't do it justice. It's classy yet playful, and it's set up so that everyone feels important, whether they're in VIP or regular seats. I love it.

"What do you think of the club?" Amante asks, brushing his lips on my ear, causing me to shiver slightly. He chuckles at my reaction. This man is going to be the end of me.

"It's perfect. I don't know what I was expecting, but it definitely wasn't this."

"Just don't fall for one of the dancers," he growls in my ear, making me shiver again.

I laugh. "I don't do love."

"That's cause you haven't met the right man...until now."

Deep down, I know he's right. No matter

how much I wanted Rex to be that man, he wasn't. There's a reason I kept things casual with men after I left Rex. No feelings, nothing to hurt. Now I'm not so sure. All those red flags I ignored with Rex aren't there with Amante.

"Why don't you get up there and dance too?" I ask him.

He laughs a full hearty laugh. "Baby, you'll never see me up there taking my clothes off."

"Why not?" I tease.

"What I have is for you only," he says in a low voice.

Holy fuck, he's sexy. Only for me? Remember that wall I constructed to keep feelings out? I can see him through it. Dammit. No one's supposed to be able to get through. I have to protect myself.

Liam

It's hard to watch my girl up on stage with Keegan. Even though all of them know she's off-fucking-limits. She doesn't know they know, but *they* know. Her hands on them is driving me fucking crazier than anything I've ever had to deal with. I want to walk away, but I can't. I may have to kick Keegan in the balls, though. Because he's touching her way too much.

"You know he's fucking with you, right?" Rónán laughs at the look on my face.

"What do you mean? He does this with all the women."

"Don't you see him looking over here?"

"Then he's being a dick." I frown. "He knows I *will* kick his ass, right?"

Rónán laughs more, and loud enough that the women sitting closest to us turn and look.

"I'm ignoring you now," I say to Rónán which makes him laugh again. Asshole.

I do love the smile on my girl's face, but I hate that it's not me that's making her smile like that.

"Love looks good on you," Luciana says, coming up beside me.

"Shut up. I'm not in love." I sigh at her.

"I've known you my whole life, Amante. You're in love. Charmaine is your person, and that makes me so happy. You know you can put in for a job change. You don't have to be my bodyguard now that you have her."

I know she's right about the job, but I can also hear a tinge of sadness in her voice.

"I'm not leaving you, Luciana, so you can get that shit out of your head right now," I growl.

"Then at least admit you love her." She smiles at me.

"You're a pain in my ass." I grab her in a headlock.

She's giggling and poking me in my side. I could never stop guarding Luciana. She's not just a job. She's my sister. We almost lost her once. If it happened again and I wasn't there? I couldn't handle that.

I finally get to spend some time with Charmaine because Rónán is now by Luciana's side. He mingles with the patrons but never strays far from her. In fact, I don't think he can handle being away from her for long. I'm beginning to understand that feeling. I don't wander far from them, but I can still pay some attention to my girl.

"Hey, beautiful. Are you enjoying yourself?" I say as I wrap my arms around her.

"It's been fun, but I like being able to spend some time with you more," she says.

I turn her to face me and lower my head to kiss her. I run my tongue over her lips as she opens to let me in. Fuck, this has to be what heaven is like. Now I understand why my mam gave up when my da died. For once I'm glad the club is loud, there's nothing we need to say in the moment that we can't say with our bodies.

While I'm wrapped up in my girl, a commotion is starting at the bar. It takes me a minute to realize it's not going to solve itself.

"Stay here," I say to Charmaine and her girls.

I head over to where the disturbance is and see my brothers getting there at the same time.

"What the fuck are you doing here?" some guy is yelling at a woman. I can't place him, but he looks familiar.

"Stop yelling at me! I'm here with my friends and you're fucking embarrassing me!" she screams back at him.

"Hey, you two are going to have to take this outside," I say to them as Granchio comes up on one side of me and Bestia on the other. The others are standing close by in case they're needed.

"Fuck you, dude. You think you're a big man standing here? This is my girl, so get the fuck out of my face. Hey, I know you. You're the shithead who thinks he can tell me what to do with Charmaine," Rex spits out.

Fucking hell. That's why he looks familiar, he's Charmaine's douchecanoe ex. At least he doesn't know she's here. He's focused on the woman he's yelling at.

"Who are you?" I ask the woman.

"I'm Sabrina, his EX girlfriend," she answers.

"'Ex my ass, Sabrina. Get out of here. Now!" Rex yells.

"Look man, she doesn't want to go with you, so why don't you just leave and cool off. Talk to her later." I try to reason with Rex. I notice he's shaking a little, like he's on something. That's not fucking good. He turns to look at me and spots Charmaine. Shit.

"Fuck her. I see my baby over there. She'll come home with me," he says, taking a step forward.

Fucking hell she will.

"Leave now or you won't like what happens next," I lean in and say to him.

Something cold and hard suddenly jabs me in the chest. It feels like the business end of a gun —I hope I'm wrong.

"Touch me and I'll kill you," he snarls, pushing me back with the muzzle of the gun he's pulled out of nowhere.

I hate being right sometimes. I put my hands up in the universal gesture of surrender to try and get him to calm him. My brothers and sisters have their guns drawn already. But pulling mine out is impossible at the moment.

"You're not taking Charmaine. So you have one other option. Drop the gun and wait for the police that are already on their way," Bestia says from beside me.

Rex laughs like a hyena. "You think you can stop me? Please." He shoots a random woman in the leg. I'm guessing to prove a point. Fuck.

I rush him as he swivels to point the gun at Charmaine and the gun goes off. I feel a heavy impact on my chest, like someone hit me with a baseball bat. Falling backwards, I see my brothers taking him down. And I hear Rex yelling that Charmaine will always be his, then another shot.

Then Charmaine is by my side pressing her hand on my chest and Luciana has a hand on my shoulder. The burning sensation is incredible.

"Please stay with me," Charmaine cries. "Please."

"Come on Liam, don't you close your fucking eyes. I don't care what, keep those damn eyes open," Luciana says to me. It must be bad, she doesn't usually call me Liam. Shit.

As hard as I try to keep my eyes open, I just can't and I start to drift. I can still hear them yelling at me but it's getting softer.

Chapter Eight

Charmaine

It's been a week since Rex shot Amante and he hasn't woken up yet. Rex is in jail, bond denied. Good. I hope he rots in there. When I realized that it was Rex yelling at Sabrina, I started to panic and run over to Amante. But Luciana stopped me. She told me that it would be bad if he had to worry about me and deal with the situation at the same time. I knew she was right so I stayed with her.

Then I saw Rex pull that gun out, shoot a random woman, then aim it towards Amante. I don't know when Amante had stepped in front of Rex, but the next thing I remember is watching him go down. Time stopped and my entire world collapsed.

When we kissed at the club, I wanted to tell him all my secrets right then. But I never got the chance. The only good thing to come out of this is I've gotten to know his MC family. Every one of them has welcomed me and my girls with open arms. It's made waiting a little easier. Luciana has told me so many stories about Amante. They grew up together. She's such a great person and I can see why Amante says they're more than just an MC.

"Please wake up, Liam. I was wrong to think we couldn't be together. I need you to wake up so I can tell you everything," I whisper to him as I sniffle.

There's no response from him, not even an eyelid twitch.

"You should go home and rest," Luciana says, coming up beside Amante's bed.

"I can't leave him. What if he wakes up? I need to be here."

"Okay, how about this—I'll clear everyone out, and you get in that shower. And I'll send

Granchio out for food. Real food. None of this hospital crap."

I look over at Luciana. See? She's awesome. I know she's just as worried about him as I am, but she's making sure I'm okay and taking care of myself.

"That would be great. Thank you."

She comes over and gives me a hug. "Do you need clothes? I could ask Vi to get you some?"

"Yeah, I could use some clean clothes. Again, thank you."

Luciana ushers everyone out of the room so I can shower. Granchio is off to get us food, and Vi is getting me some clothes.

Before I get into the shower, I make sure to talk to Amante.

"I'm not leaving you, I just need to grab a quick shower. I'll be as fast as I can so that when you wake up, I'll be here," I whisper to him. I kiss his lips, still waiting for some sign that he's waking up. But nothing happens.

I take the fastest shower ever, because what if he wakes up while I'm in here? I can't let him wake up alone. The hot water helps me relax a little and I start thinking about what a life with Amante would be like. Maybe we could even have a family together. The world needs little Amantes in it. As I'm getting out, I hear a knock on the door. I dry off and wrap the towel around me.

"Hey Charmy, it's Vi. I have your clothes."

"You can come in," I reply. "Thank you so much for doing this."

She comes over and hugs me.

"I need him to wake up, Vi. Why won't he wake up?" I sniffle.

"I don't know, sis. But what I do know is that he will. You just keep doing what you're doing and it'll be okay."

I hug her back tightly.

"I'm going back out there, you get dressed. Are they still giving you time off work?" she asks.

"Yeah, it seems the Mancinis and Bastianinis are pretty close, so they're giving me paid time off. I was told to take as much time as I need."

"That's so awesome. I'm glad they're being so understanding."

I nod at her. "Me too."

"What if he doesn't want me after knowing everything I let happen with Rex?" I whisper to her.

"Get it right, little sister. What Rex did to

you was in no way your fault. He's an asshole, and he took advantage of your love. You left when you could; that doesn't make you weak."

"But I should've seen it earlier. I was so convinced he was 'the one' that I ignored all the red flags."

"That's not your fault, you were just trying to see the best in him. So stop blaming yourself. When you tell Liam about what happened, he'll make sure you never feel like that again."

"How do you know? I thought I had that with Rex. What if we're wrong again?"

"My gut is telling me that he's the one for you, and you just need to trust yourself again."

I know she's right, my gut has been telling me that from the moment we met. I've been ignoring it out of fear. Well, that's going to stop. It has to if I'm ever going to be happy again.

She leaves so I can get dressed, and I hear more voices coming into the room. I'm guessing that Granchio is back with food and everyone has come back with him. I love how the whole club has been here for Amante. It's made me feel less alone. My girls have been by every day to check on us. I love them so much.

Liam

I feel like I'm floating. Every once in a while I hear Charmaine's sweet voice talking to me. But for some reason I can't wake up and answer her. I've heard Luciana too, telling me that I need to find my way back to them. If only I knew how to do that.

Voices are louder right now, I can hear my club family talking. I try to open my eyes, but I can't seem to do it. It's like I don't have control over them. Then there's moving my body. I can't seem to do that either. I feel someone holding my hand, and then I hear Charmaine talking to me. I think it's her holding my hand, but I can't get my eyes open. What the fuck.

Charmaine

"We're going to reduce Liam's pain medication. I think that will help him wake up," Doctor Turner says.

"But won't that mean he'll be in more pain?" I ask.

"Yes, that's a possibility. But I feel the high dosage might be keeping his body from knowing it's time to wake up," he explains.

"Is Giacomo Bastianini here? He needs to sign the papers for us to change Liam's meds."

Luciana told me that Giacomo is Liam's medical proxy—and has been since his parents passed away, in case of emergencies.

"I'm here," Giacomo says in his rumbly voice. "Are you sure we aren't harming him by doing this?"

"There's no real way to know. Only Liam can tell us what he's feeling when he wakes up. And when he does, if he needs more pain medication, I'll give it to him."

"Okay, Doc." He sighs and reads the paper the doctor gives him. I guess it's okay with him because he signs it. And the doctor starts to lower the amount of meds that are flowing into Amante. Please let this work.

"It could take up to twenty-four hours for him to wake up," Doctor Turner says.

"Okay thanks, Doc," Giacomo says.

After the doctor and nurse leave, he turns to me.

"I'm going to leave Granchio here with you. And there's a police officer stationed right outside the door. The rest of us will head home and try to get some sleep. We'll be back first thing in the morning," he says.

"Okay, thank you so much." I make sure to hug everyone before they leave.

Chapter Nine

Liam

There's a prickly feeling running down my body. I'm finally able to unglue my eyelids and slowly open them. Looking over to my left in the dimly lit room, I see my beautiful Charmaine. She's curled up on a cot, snoring softly. I want to wake her, but she looks exhausted.

I hear someone whisper, "Hey, brother."

I turn my head slowly to the other side and see Granchio. He looks just as tired, but there's relief on his face.

"How...long?" I rasp out. Trying to talk feels like I'm swallowing sandpaper.

Granchio quietly brings over a cup and adds water to it. I sip it slowly through a straw.

"It's been a little over a week. Do you remember what happened?"

I nod yes. "She okay?" I turn my head towards Charmaine.

"She's good and hasn't left your side." He smiles at me.

I close my eyes as I nod at him.

"Liam?" I slowly move my hand towards her voice. "Thank God you're awake." She starts crying.

I pull her to me and try to get her to lie down on the bed.

"I'll hurt you." She sobs.

"No," is all I can say as I gently tug on her hand. She finally gives in and carefully lies down next to me, laying her head on my chest.

"I was so scared," she whispers.

Granchio slips out the door to give us some privacy. And to call everyone, if I had to guess. I don't know the extent of my injuries, I just know that when Rex pointed that gun at me, then my girl...I saw red and attacked him as he pulled the trigger. I remember him yelling that she will always be his. Then he fired again, and everything went dark.

"I'm okay, baby," I say slowly. My mouth is still acting like it doesn't know how to work.

"I need you in my life, Liam. I'm so sorry I thought we could never be together. I was a coward and so afraid. But I'm not anymore, I just hope I'm not too late to tell you." She sniffles.

"Never too late, I would've waited forever for you," I whisper.

She holds me a little tighter and I wrap my arms around her as best I can. She's finally mine. And as soon as I can get the fuck out of this damn hospital bed, I'll show her exactly what that means.

After a few minutes, the doctor comes in with Granchio on his heels.

"I see we're awake," the doctor says, smiling. "How is your pain on a scale of one to ten?"

"Six or seven."

He nods. "If you feel like you need more pain meds, let us know and we'll adjust it again. For tonight, I want you to rest. Tomorrow the work starts. I want you up and walking. Even a week of no real movement can affect your joints and muscles."

"Okay, Doc." I nod.

"I'll be in tomorrow morning. I'm glad you're awake."

"Thanks." I smile.

"I'll be outside, everyone said they'll be here bright and early. And to make sure I tell you they're so happy you're awake," Granchio says.

"Thanks, brother."

Granchio sniffles softly and walks out of the room.

"Thank you for staying with me," I say, kissing Charmaine's head.

"You're my home, Liam, my safe place. I'm so sorry it took you getting hurt for me to snap out of my shit and admit it."

"Don't ever be sorry. Tell me why you've been so scared. What did Rex do to you?"

Charmaine

Taking a deep breath, I begin to tell Amante what I went through with Rex.

"I suppose we're not going anywhere. Which is good because this is going to be a long one," I mumble.

"I'm here for it all, Charmaine. There's nothing you could tell me that would change the way I feel about you."

For the first time since leaving Rex, I feel safe enough to let someone in. To confess everything that happened.

"At the beginning things were great. He was my first boyfriend, my first everything."

Amante growls softly at my admission of giving Rex my firsts.

"About six months in, we got into a huge fight at a party. He kept flirting with this girl. He went so far as to kiss her and when I confronted him, he kept apologizing, saying it was the booze. And that he would never do it again, of course. I was an idiot and believed him."

"You're not an idiot, we all want to believe the best about the people we love. He took advantage of that."

"Maybe. I should've listened to my gut and left him then. But I was afraid of being alone, so I gave him another chance. The next time I caught him was through a text. He sent me a text saying how much fun he had the night before and he couldn't wait to see me again. The thing is, we lived together, so I knew it wasn't meant for me."

I take a few breaths, trying not to start crying again. Rex doesn't deserve my tears. Amante stays quiet and tightens his hold on me.

"When I confronted him about the text, he

said I was acting jealous and needed to let it go. That I was assuming it was for another girl, when in reality it was for his buddy that needed help wording a text to a girl he liked. I pushed harder, and he ended up hitting me for the first time. Of course, the next morning he kept apologizing and said he was just so angry because I didn't trust him. Then came the promises of never touching me like that again. It lasted for about six more months. Everything was great, and it felt like we were finally on the right track."

Amantes tenses up, like he knows the worst is yet to come. He's not wrong.

"This was about two years into our relationship. I had to work late at the Grill because a server had called out. I needed the extra money, so I said I would stay. It was about one a.m. by the time I walked in the door. The first thing I saw were the dishes. It looked like someone had cooked a meal for two. At first I was happy cause I thought maybe it was for me. Then I noticed the two used wine glasses and the plates that had been eaten off of. I quietly made my way to our bedroom and found him in the middle of having sex with the same girl that had called off work. Her name was Sabrina, and she had been working with me for almost a year at that point."

"Jesus," Amante whispers.

"I remember her making him stop when she saw me. Then she scrambled to grab her clothes and ran out. Rex just stared at me, then before I could react, he pounced on me. He was screaming that since I interrupted his time with Sabrina, he would take it out on me. He tied me to the bed and alternated between raping and beating me. I woke up three days later in the hospital."

"Why the fuck isn't he in jail?" Amante says through clenched teeth.

"Because when he was done, I had already passed out. So he called the police and told them he found me like that. He even made it look like someone had broken in. And it didn't help that his best friend is a detective on the force."

"And Sabrina? Please tell me she backed you up."

I shake my head no. "She backed *him* up and said he was at her place all night."

"Does she still work at the Grill?" he asks.

"God no, after Giovanna Mancini found out that Sabrina was cheating with Rex, she fired her. She said that's something that would never be tolerated in their businesses. That it showed how little Sabrina respected me. I know Sabrina tried to sue the Mancinis for wrongful termination. But she failed to read some of the fine print in the paperwork we sign when we're hired. It basically says that if you're found to disrespect any other employee, the owners can either put you on probation or fire you."

"Good. If she ever bothers you, you let me know." He frowns.

"I thought she was still with Rex, but at the club, Luciana said she heard Sabrina say Rex was her ex. So I'm not sure what their deal is. Last I heard she was living with him. And I don't know if she knows about him stalking me."

"Well, she's definitely not a bright one. Now finish your story so I can help you heal."

"It took me a few weeks to come up with a plan. Rex told me that if I tried to leave him or tell anyone what really happened, he would make sure I was never found. Vi and the girls helped me. Rex had to go away for business, and was supposed to be gone for five days. We had planned to get my stuff packed and be out before he got back. We were almost done when he walked in a day early. He tried to stop us, but Lila had called the police as soon as she saw him pull into the driveway. So when the police showed up, they stayed until I got the rest of my stuff out and helped me file a report. That way, I could get a restraining order started that day. He's never followed the restraining order, but he doesn't get violent with me anymore. What he does is what you saw the night we met. He'll show up wherever I am and threaten me or try to get me to leave with him."

"He's never going to come near you again. And if he does? I'm the one you call," he says, looking at me.

"Okay," I say, giving him a kiss. "Now you need to rest, I have a feeling once everyone shows back up, you won't get to do much resting."

He chuckles. "You're probably right. But I want you right here, so don't even think about moving."

We both fall asleep for the next few hours, only waking when we hear everyone start to come in.

Chapter Ten

Liam

It took two weeks to get the all clear from the doctor so I could go home. It's crazy how much muscle mass you can lose from being immobile for less than two weeks. Luckily, this is something Rónán knows a lot about, so he's been helping me with meals and light exercise. Next week I'll be able to hit the gym again.

Charmaine still hasn't left my side and I'm not complaining one bit. But I know she's eager to get back to work too. She loves her job, and I hate that she's missing it because of me.

"You know you can go back to work if you

want, baby. I'll have one of the brothers go with you."

"Go with me? Why?" she asks.

"I don't want you without a bodyguard. None of the women go anywhere without one. And you're no different," I answer.

"I have you, I don't need a bodyguard."

"Please don't argue with me on this. One of my brothers will be with you when I'm not. If I could be with you all the time, I would. But I can't. Once I'm cleared, my job is to guard Luciana."

"I forgot about that. I got spoiled having you with me all the time." She sighs.

"You know you have nothing to worry about with her, right?"

"Oh, I know. I love her and all the women in your family. I just didn't think about when you'd have to go back to 'normal' life."

I wrap my arms around her. "You are my 'normal' life, amore."

I kiss her with everything I have; I don't want her doubting anything. Her moans are my undoing. As I run my hands down her body, she arches her back at my touch.

"I need you, Liam. Please," she moans.

I had been holding back because I didn't want to push her.

"Anything you want, baby," I say as I slowly take her shirt off.

Fuck. It's been so long since I've been with anyone. I need to make sure I take care of her. I nip at her through her bra as I slide my hand down her body.

"You're fucking perfect, Charmaine."

She kisses my chest, sliding her hand down my stomach, "No. You first, amore," I growl as I unhook her bra. After taking a minute to look at her beautiful breasts, I slowly lick one into a stiff peak and then work on the other. Hearing her moan is driving me crazy. My cock is weeping and demanding to be let in on the fun.

"Liam..." She gasps.

I run my tongue down her belly and slide her jeans off. "Fucking perfect," I say again as I use my teeth to get her underwear off. I take a moment to breathe her in and look at what's finally mine. I'm in fucking heaven. I bite her inner thigh and am rewarded with a gasp. I slowly lick her slit from bottom to the top and suck on her clit.

"Fuck." She moans.

I slide one finger in, then a second as I work

her towards the first of many orgasms she'll be having tonight.

"Please, I need to feel you." She moans more.

I smile and stand up. I peel my shirt off and revel in the lust that's rolling off her in waves. Then I slowly take my belt and jeans off, leaving my boxer briefs on to tease her.

"Stop fucking teasing me," she growls.

I give her another smile and take off the last thing standing between us. I stroke myself a few times and watch her eyes follow my hand. Then I position myself over her.

"Do I need protection? Because if you want me to, I'll put one on. I've never had unprotected sex, ever. But I want to feel all of you, and you to feel all of me," I say as I rub myself on her slit.

"I'm clean. After...well after that happened, I got all the tests and I've never gone without protection since," she whispers. "I want to feel all of you."

That's what I needed to hear from my girl. I slowly push into her. I'm not a small man, so I make sure she's okay. But fuck me, I want to just seat myself to the hilt and live there. I finally push fully in and holy fuck. Please don't let me embarrass myself.

I begin to move, and she grabs my ass, making me move faster. Fuck.

"I don't think I'm going to last, baby. I need you to come with me." I gasp, running my hand down between us and circling her clit.

"Fuck." She gasps as she explodes, clenching my cock so hard it feels like a vice, squeezing the cum out of me.

We lay there panting for what feels like hours.

"Jesus, baby." I chuckle.

Charmaine

"If I knew it was going to be that good, I wouldn't have waited so long." I giggle.

Liam laughs and pulls me tighter to him.

"It's never been that fucking good with anyone," he says.

I nod. Because no one has ever made me feel the way he does, physically or emotionally. He's my person. My soulmate.

"For me too," I whisper. I'm no longer afraid of giving Liam my heart. He's shown me in more ways than one how much I mean to him. I'm finally able to see a future with someone. A future that includes a whole second family, and when we decide to have babies, they'll be surrounded by so much love. This is a dream I thought had died when Rex attacked me. But I won. He lost. I'm stronger now than ever.

It's been almost a month since Amante has been home and I think I'm finally ready to go back to work. I love my job and the Mancinis. Every one of them has come by to see Amante and make sure he's healing. I knew they were good people, but seeing them with the Bastianinis, it's the whole package. It's the type of family that's made by choice, not by blood. And I'm beginning to think it's the best kind. I love my blood family, but the honesty and love I feel from my chosen one sometimes surpasses them.

"I'm glad you're back, Charmy," Giovanna Mancini says when I walk into work. She gives me a big hug. That's another thing the Mancinis and Bastianinis have in common. Hugs. They believe that if you're going to hug someone, that hug should show how much that person means to you. And if they don't? Then don't hug them. I believe in that.

"Thanks, Gia. I'm ready to be back. I miss Liam, though." I chuckle.

"That man is missable." She giggles as her husband, Declan O'Reilly, star defenseman and alternate captain for the Chicago Redhawks hockey team, comes walking over. He's holding their six-month-old son, Rowan.

"Who's missable?" he teases.

She turns and gives him the biggest smile. "You, my love. You're missable."

The kiss he gives her makes even me blush. Shit. Now I miss Liam even more.

"Damn you two, now I wish I had decided to stay home another day." I laugh.

They both laugh with me. "I wish we could just stay home all the time too." Gia smiles.

"Isn't there a game tomorrow night?" I ask.

"Yes! We need to redeem ourselves after the last one." Declan sighs.

"Aww it wasn't that bad..." I trail off, looking at the floor. Because it really was that bad.

"Six to one isn't bad?" he says, making a funny noise.

"We're all diehard fans, so win or lose, it's all good." I smile at him.

"Good answer." Gia chuckles.

The rest of my night goes by fast. Which is good, cause I couldn't wait to get home to my man. My. Man. I never thought I would say that about anyone. Let alone be living with them within a couple of months. Life is seriously crazy. But I love it.

Chapter Eleven

Liam

I'm about to do something I've never wanted to do before. Not once in my whole damn life. I'm going to take my Charmy out on a date. Luciana and Isabella have been helping me plan it for the last week. Because I know *zero* about these things. I do know that I want it to be special and something she'll remember forever. And I don't want a stereotypical fancy dinner.

Charmaine makes me look forward to all the things I swore I didn't want. I finally get to have what my parents did. And it scares the ever-loving shit out of me. What if I lose her? What if she decides that I'm not worth the trouble? Holy fuck, I've turned into a wuss. Thank god my club brothers can't hear what I'm thinking.

I look at the clothes that Luciana picked out for me. A deep blue button-down shirt that she said will bring out the light gray swirlies in my eyes. Whatever the fuck that means. And a pair of black jeans. I'm not allowed to wear a hat—I'm not sure why, and that annoys me. My hair is wavy and I have to use shit to make it behave. I hate it, so I wear hats.

"This is for my girl," I repeat to myself while I finish getting ready. I grab my cut as I walk out the door.

Walking to my bike, I hear catcalls and whistles. Fuck. My brothers are out and watching me. Why? Assholes.

"Looking good, Amante! Living up to your name, huh?" Ombra yells as he laughs. I flip him off and do my best to ignore him.

"You look wonderful." I turn and see Caitríona standing there. She gives me a hug only a mam can give.

"Thank you, Forte." I smile.

"Oh come on, nights like tonight I'm 'Caitríona' or 'Mam'. We all know this," she says softly.

And she's right. After my da passed, Giacomo and Caitríona stepped in to help my mam and me. Then, when I lost my mam, they embraced me even more.

I hug her tight. "Thank you for being here for me."

"The club isn't the only reason you're important to us, Liam. We would never have trusted you with Luciana's life if we didn't trust you as part of our family. I miss your parents too. All the time."

Hearing her say that makes me miss my parents even more. They would've loved Charmaine and I wish they were both around to meet her. But I'm grateful for my MC family and everything they've given me.

"Your parents would be so proud of the man you've become. And you know they're always watching over you. Charmaine is great, and she's perfect for you. And when you're ready, we'll welcome her into the family for good."

I sniffle a little, trying not to turn into a blubbering wuss puddle. Instead of replying, I just hug her tighter. She makes missing my mam little easier, and I know how much my mam loved Caitríona too.

Okay, time to leave and show my woman how much I cherish her.

Charmaine

All I know about tonight is I was told to dress comfortably. What does that even mean? A sundress? Jeans? What kind of instructions are these? Okay fine, I'm freaking myself out, probably over nothing. My girls are here helping me, along with Luciana and Isabella. I know the twins know what's going on and they're not telling. In fact, I think they all know and they're all assholes for keeping it a secret.

Luciana picks out a blouse and jeans for me to wear. Then presents me with a box she's brought with her.

"You're going to be on the bike with him, so a dress isn't a good idea," she says. "We all pitched in and bought you this."

I take the box and open it. It's a beautiful leather jacket.

"Since you're a bike-riding badass now, you need leather to protect you." She smiles.

"But I'm just a passenger. I'm too chicken to ride alone."

"Passenger or not, you need the proper gear. That's why Amante bought you a helmet and riding boots. He knew we had already got you the jacket," Isabella says.

"Thank you, all of you, for everything."

We do a big group hug. I love how my girls have become friends with Luciana and Isabella. We've also met their friends and have gotten together to do things. I have an even bigger tribe now, and it's more than I could've ever hoped for. And I have my big bad biker man, who's tough when he needs to be, but so tender and loving with me.

"Okay, someone spill it about tonight." I squint at them one by one.

They all look away and ignore me like they did when I asked earlier. Again. Assholes. Tender moment is over.

"I hear rumbly noises." Faith giggles as she looks out of the window. "Yup, your muscley man is here."

The rumbling stops and we hear a knock at the door.

"I'll get it." Luciana laughs. "Hey Liam, looking good. Charmaine's going to love it."

Luciana steps aside and I see my dream man. I've never seen anyone who can wear literally anything and look as sexy as he does.

"These are for you, amore," he says, handing me a beautiful bouquet of roses and tulips, then giving me a kiss.

"Thank you." I smile.

"I'll take those and put them in a vase. You two go, have fun and be safe," Chloe says.

They all push us out the door. "You know this is my apartment, right?" I laugh.

"Yeah yeah yeah." They laugh as we leave.

Liam

"So are you going to tell me what the surprise is?" Charmaine asks as we walk to my bike.

"Nope. A surprise means you see it when it's time. It's not time yet." I chuckle.

She pouts at me and I kiss her, putting my helmet on before she can respond. "Pout all you want, baby. I'm a vault with surprises."

She sighs and puts her new helmet on, then we sync our headsets so we can talk while we ride. After that, I help her onto my bike and wait for her to get situated to start it up. I love the rumble it makes, it's a sound that soothes my soul. It's also a sound that has always reminded me of my parents.

"You look sexy in leather," I say to her. I can hear her giggle into the headset.

"Thank you for my helmet and boots, they fit perfectly. And I was so surprised when the girls gave me the jacket. I feel like a real biker chick now."

"You *are* a real biker chick, baby. *My* biker chick."

I'm taking her to a pond on the clubhouse property. I want to introduce her to the otters. The otter family that lives there has been with us for almost seven months now. The original otter family lives with our MC in Ireland. Francesco wanted to have otters here for his daughter. But because he couldn't bring the Irish otters here to Chicago, it took some time and research. We had all kinds of experts come out to make sure we had the proper space for them. I know it doesn't seem romantic to take her to the MC property. But for what I have planned, it's perfect.

I park my bike on the far side of the pond, across the way from the houses. We can see the lights coming from them, and they cast a glow across the water.

"What are we doing here?" Charmaine asks, smiling at me.

"You'll see." I chuckle, grabbing the blanket and basket that's strapped to my bike. I lay the blanket down at the edge of the pond and start unpacking the basket. Luciana made sure we had an assortment of sandwiches, chips, veggies and fruit. The veggies and fruit are mostly for the otters. I pat the blanket next to me and she comes over to sit down.

We sit in comfortable silence for a few minutes, then the otters start popping up out of the water.

"The otters! I thought you were joking about them being here!" She starts laughing as they climb all over her. Charmaine's laugh is the best sound. She laughs with her whole body, and I love it.

I hand her veggies and fruit to feed the otters. Some take them and eat with us, and some take their loot back to the water.

"Can we swim with them in the pond?" she asks.

"Yep. This is the smaller pond so they like it better. The bigger pond over there is where we use the jet skis and keep the smaller boats. This pond is actually big enough for jet skis but we worry about the otters," I explain.

"That makes sense. Maybe we can come back and swim with them one day?"

"Of course. You can come and swim with them anytime."

We spend a few hours hanging with the otters and just talking. It's the best date I've ever had. Well, the only date.

"Thank you for all this, Liam. And thank you for being so patient with me. After everything that happened with Rex, I truly felt that avoiding relationships was the way to go. But you've shown me that I was right the first time. There *is* someone for us out there, and sometimes we just have to sift through the shit to find the diamond."

I lean down and capture her lips, hearing her moan as I deepen the kiss. I lean back and look into her eyes.

"I spent most of my life believing that one night was enough, but you made me see that there's more. I can't wait to spend the rest of my life with you. You deserve everything in this world and I plan to be the one to give it all to you. I love you, Charmaine."

"I love you too, Liam. So damn much."

Epilogue

Liam

We're doing a karaoke night at the clubhouse. We've invited Charmaine's family and all the Mancinis. It's going to be a great night. I'm also going to be doing two things that I never thought I would ever do. The first is less scary than the second. But I hope they both turn out alright.

It's been two months since that night at the club. Rex will be going on trial for two counts of aggravated assault and illegal possession of a gun. He's facing up to four years for each assault and another seven for the gun possession. We're hoping he gets consecutive sentences. That will mean that he serves one after another and we could be free of him for up to fifteen years.

Charmaine

"What's going on? Where's Amante?" Vi asks me.

I shrug my shoulders. "I don't know, all I know is that everyone is here, including mom and dad."

"Oh my god. I bet he's going to propose!" she screams.

"Shush, Vi." Again, I need a new sister. There's no way Liam is going to propose tonight, I mean we've talked about it but that's it. Talk.

Luciana gets up in front of everyone.

"Hey everyone, in case you don't know who I am, I'm Luciana Bastianini."

"Soon to be O'Callaghan!" Rónán yells and everyone laughs.

"This is true." She smiles. "But that's for another day. Today is special and anyone who knows me knows how important family is to me. I have two sometimes-awesome older brothers and one kick-ass sister. What people don't realize is that we grew up with another brother. He's not blood, but he's no less our brother. Tonight he'll be doing something I've been asking him to do in public since we were teenagers. But it took a special woman for him to finally say yes."

I can hear murmurs from the crowd. They're trying to figure out what Liam is going to do. That includes me, because I have no idea.

"I also need Giovanna Mancini up here for this," Luciana says. She hugs Gia as she joins her up front.

We watch as they set up two stools and two microphones. I know Gia sings, I've heard her and she's got a beautiful voice. Liam sings around the house and I love listening to him. His voice soothes me in ways I can't even describe.

Speaking of Liam...he's walking out on stage with a guitar, then takes a seat next to Gia. She picks up her guitar and waits for him.

"I've never done this before, so please bear with me. About two months ago, I met a woman that made me believe in everything I swore I wouldn't. My parents were soulmates and when we lost my da, my mam tried to hang on. But she just couldn't live without him. And as much as it hurt, I understood. That made me swear off relationships. Why put your heart out there just to lose it? Then I met Charmaine Holt. My Charmy. And everything went out the window. She absolutely crushed all my fears and showed me so many possibilities. And she's just as stubborn as me, which makes things interesting," Amante says and chuckles. "So this song's for you —my heart, my love, my future. It's called "Nobody But You" by Blake Shelton. It says everything I could ever want to say to you."

Before he even starts singing, tears are streaming down my face. I can hear sniffling all around me, even the big bad bikers are wiping their eyes. This man is so much more than I ever could have wished for. I'm thankful for him everyday.

As he's getting to the end of the song, he puts his guitar down, takes his microphone and walks to me. When he finishes the song, he gets down on one knee.

"Charmaine. I never wanted to meet you because that meant I had the chance of losing you. But now that I have? I wouldn't have it any other way. I'll never give you up. I can't say I won't make mistakes, but I'll always make it better. That I can promise you. I love you. Will you marry me?" he says with tears shining in his eyes. My big bad biker is tearing up, asking me to marry him.

"Yes, Liam. Yes. It'll always be you and me, now and forever," I say with my own tears falling.

He picks me up and swings me around. Everyone is cheering and hugging us.

Two years ago I thought my life was done, that I was too broken to fix. I thought I would be alone forever.

Today, I have a fiancé and a family by choice.

Notchin' Boots Series

I hope you enjoyed Amante and Charmaine's story!

These women own their sexuality and aren't ashamed of the notches on their bedposts. Will the heroes who come into their lives be enough to show them how good commitment can be and get these ladies to throw out their little black books? Join some of your favorite romance authors for the Notchin' Boots Series and find out this February.

Grab the entire series here

Another Notch on the Bartop by Ember Davis

Notch Afraid by Jade Royal

Notch the Plan by Natalie Arthur

Notch Yours by Haven Rose

<u>Another Notch On Her Toolbelt</u> by Euryia Larsen

<u>All or Notching</u> by Anne Lange

<u>Notching Her Up</u> by Autumn Wilds

<u>Notching The Line</u> by Layne Daniels

Hi! I'm Natalie. I published my first book, Aftermath in August 2021. I've been lucky enough to find my own insta-love-at-first-sight person. We have a daughter who drives us crazy and a corgi who adds to the chaos. I love hockey (Chicago Blackhawks), MotoGP (Motorcycle Racing), and baseball (Chicago Cubs). When I'm not writing, you can find me studying or crafting. Or crafting when I should be studying.

Nataliearthurbooks.com

hockey players. But I want to trust someone again...
maybe he's the one?

<u>Declan</u>

Hockey has been my focus for as long as I can remember. The day I met Giovanna, my life changed. Hockey would always be my first love. But she would be my last. Something happened to her and she's afraid to trust me. But that's okay, I'll show her that I'm real. That we're real.

Aftermath is the first book in my Mancini Legacy Series. All books are standalone, but it's best if read in order. There is mention of characters from my Cimaruta MC Chicago Series.

https://books2read.com/Aftermath-ManciniLegacy

<u>Sebastiano</u>

I had given up on meeting my person, content to be the protector of my family. Then one day I met her. But someone else was laying claim to her. If she was happy, I would step back and watch her from afar. But then I saw the marks on her and I knew I needed to save her.

<u>Schuyler</u>

It seems like I've been struggling most of my life. Just my sister and me against the world. Then I thought I met the man of my dreams. Turns out he's the man from my nightmares. I can't run and I can't escape from him. Then I met Sebastiano. He made me feel safe from the moment he took my hand in his. He says I will be his, but he doesn't know about the monster that's in my life. The one that won't let go.

Saving Her is the second book in my Mancini Legacy Series. All books are standalone, but it's best if read in order. There is mention of characters from my Cimaruta MC Chicago Series.

https://books2read.com/SavingHer-ManciniLegacy

<u>Luciana</u>

Women on an MC council? It's unheard of until now. Love at first sight? That's a new one for me too. I was convinced I didn't need someone to make me happy.

Then I slammed into Rónán.

Literally.

In an instant, he turned my world upside down. But can he handle the MC life?

<u>Rónán</u>

My life was going the way I planned it. Then the most beautiful woman stepped into my path and changed my life forever. I know she's keeping things from me. And that's okay...for now.

Because she's mine.

She just doesn't know it yet.

Choices is the first book in my Cimaruta MC Chicago Series. All books are standalone, but it's best if read in order. There is mention of characters from my Mancini Legacy Series.

https://books2read.com/Choices-CimarutaMCChicago

Francesco

I met the love of my life at fourteen. She had my heart the moment I saw her. But when you're young and stupid you don't always make the right decisions. That's what happened to me. I let the temptations of my job distract me from the one thing I couldn't live without. I had lost all hope, but fate gave me another chance. I have to make it up to her. I know she's hiding something from me. Will she let me in and give me a second chance?

<u>**Maeve**</u>

I thought I had it all. Sure I may have been young, but when it's real, you just know. That was, until he ended things. I never saw it coming. Now he's back and he wants another chance. Can I really trust him not to break my heart again? I want to believe him. I've never stopped loving him. But it's not just me I have to protect anymore.

Can they find their way back to the happily ever after they were meant to have? Or will they be pulled apart again, shattering all hope?

Reclaiming Our Forever is the second book in my Cimaruta MC Chicago Series. All books are standalone, but it's best if read in order. There is mention of characters from my Mancini Legacy Series.

https://books2read.com/ReclaimingOurForever-CimarutaMCChicago

Hollis

The people you're born to don't always turn out to be your 'family'. Families can be chosen, and I chose the Cimaruta MC. They've been there with me for the last six years, and I thought I had everything I needed. One night was all it took to make me want more. But she's hiding something from me and I need to know what it is. I will save her from anything. That much I do know.

Lila

My life was finally going smoothly. It was me and my

daughter against the world. I worked at a club called Club Curve—I'm a curvy girl, so why not? Then one night, HE walked in. Now he's turning my life upside down and I'm not sure how to feel about it. My biggest fear is about to become a reality.

Just as you are is a stand alone and part of the Club Curve series. But there is mention of characters from my Mancini Legacy and Cimaruta MC Chicago series.

https://books2read.com/JustAsYouAre-ClubCurve

<u>Kostas</u>

Mating matches keep the peace in our world. So why did it feel like my life was over when it was my turn? She hated me from the moment we were paired. And to be honest? I hated her too. So when she rejected me for some loser from another clan, it didn't bother me that much. But then I met her—the one the fates chose for me—and everything just felt right. I knew in an instant that she was the one I would never let go of.

<u>Artemis</u>

In our world, mates can be either fated or chosen, but finding your fated mate is never guaranteed. I thought I had chosen someone who could love me and we would spend our lives together. But then he rejected me—for my BEST FRIEND. That day, I decided I was fine being alone. But then, completely by chance, I met someone who felt like home. Could this really be it? The forever I secretly craved...my fated one.

My Fated One is part of the Fated Mates Series. There is mention of characters from my Mancini Legacy Series and my Cimaruta MC Chicago Series.

https://books2read.com/MyFatedOne-FatedMates

Aiden

Motorcycle racing has been my life since I could walk
and talk. It was all I ever needed. Or so I thought.
Then I met the one woman that made me want more.
One day, the unthinkable happens—a racing accident
causes me to lose all my memories of her. But I still feel
her in my soul, even if my brain can't remember her.

Élodie

I wanted a knight in shining armor, but what I got was
a wolf in disguise. After escaping from him, I met a
man willing to give me everything I ever wanted. Then

in a split second, he was taken from me. Not physically, but mentally. The man I love doesn't remember who I am, but I'm determined to get him back.

Racing Back to Love is part of the Forget-Me-Not Series. There is mention of characters from my Mancini Legacy Series.

https://books2read.com/RacingBackToLove-ForgetMeNot

www.ingramcontent.com/pod-product-compliance
Lightning Source LLC
Chambersburg PA
CBHW061544310726
48972CB00008B/2597